PAUL'S SECOND JOURNEY

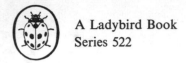

A Ladybird Book
Series 522

This book tells the story of St. Paul—of his childhood in Tarsus, his persecution of the Christians, his conversion to Christianity and his journeys taking the news of Jesus Christ to other lands.

The story of
SAINT PAUL

by D. S. HARE

with illustrations by ERIC WINTER

Publishers: Wills & Hepworth Ltd., Loughborough
First published 1969   ©   *Printed in England*

THE STORY OF SAINT PAUL

Our story begins with a young boy called Saul, who was born about the same time as Jesus. His parents were prominent Jews who held the rank of Roman citizens.

They did not live in Palestine, but in a large sea-port called Tarsus, an important trading centre on the north-east coast of the Mediterranean.

Here Saul met Arabs, Egyptians, Greeks and Romans, and learnt something of the ideas and beliefs of all these different peoples. But he also learned to love all men, of every race.

As Saul grew up, he went to the school attached to the Synagogue, the Jewish place of worship. Saul had a keen mind, and at about the age of fifteen he went to Jerusalem to study law under the famous teacher, Gamaliel. There he began his training to become a Jewish lawyer.

In Jerusalem, Saul soon showed that he was a good scholar and that he had a quick, sharp mind. At that time the Jewish Law consisted of many thousands of small rules, and the lawyers had to decide how these were to be interpreted.

The Jews believed that religion was the keeping of these laws, and that strict obedience to every rule made a person pleasing to God. Saul once claimed he had never broken a single rule.

When Saul was older, he learned that the disciples of Jesus had begun to preach that Jesus, whom the Jews had crucified, was the Son of God and had risen from the dead. They taught people to trust in Him to forgive their wrongs and that this was the only way of salvation acceptable to God.

Saul at once saw that this teaching was directly opposed to the Jewish Law, and he determined to stamp out the new religion.

Saul decided to investigate the new teaching more fully. The more he did so, the more he became convinced that the new religion must be crushed.

Some of the Pharisees, the strictest Jews, found one of the believers in Jesus, named Stephen, and asked him to explain his beliefs. This he did, reminding his hearers that many of God's prophets had been killed for proclaiming the truth. He told them that Jesus was the Messiah promised by God, and that although they had crucified Him, He had risen from the dead.

The Pharisees were very angry when they heard this, and refused to listen any longer. They dragged Stephen outside the city and began to stone him to death.

"Lord Jesus," cried Stephen, "receive my spirit, and do not hold this sin against them."

So Stephen died, and Saul approved of his death.

Saul continued to hunt out the followers of Jesus, and to persecute them. But while he was leading a party of soldiers to Damascus, to arrest and imprison any believers he found there, Saul had an experience which completely transformed his life.

While travelling along the road, he was suddenly struck down by a blinding light. He heard a voice saying to him, "Saul, Saul, why do you persecute me?"

"Who are you, Lord?" he answered.

"I am Jesus, whom you are persecuting."

"What do you want me to do, Lord?" Saul asked.

"Go into Damascus, and there you will be told what to do," was the reply.

Those who were with him heard the voice, but saw no one else. But Saul was forever afterwards certain that he had actually met Jesus.

Now, still blinded, he was led by the hand into Damascus.

In Damascus, a disciple called Ananias to whom God had already spoken, went to the house where Saul was staying. He greeted him, saying, "Brother Saul, the Lord Jesus has sent me so that you may recover your sight and be filled with the Spirit."

At once Saul was able to see again. He then went into the synagogue and preached that Jesus was the Son of God.

How surprised the people must have been! The man who had come to imprison the Christians was now preaching that they must believe in Jesus.

But some Jews were very angry. They plotted to kill Saul, and watched all day and all night at the city gates to catch him.

Saul's life was in danger, so one night the disciples let him down over the city wall in a basket! This way he escaped and returned to Jerusalem a very changed man.

At Jerusalem, Saul had difficulty in joining the Christians, who could not believe that he was a true disciple. They suspected a trick.

But Barnabas, a friend and companion, told them about Saul's conversion when he was on the way to Damascus. So Saul was allowed to join the Christians and he preached boldly about Jesus. But in Jerusalem also there were plots against his life, so he was sent back to Tarsus for safety.

Later on, Barnabas went to Tarsus to find Saul. He brought him to Antioch, in Syria, where for a whole year they met believers and taught large crowds of people. It was here that those who believed in Jesus were first given the name "Christians".

Then God called Barnabas and Saul to take the message of the good news of Jesus Christ to other lands, and to other people as well as the Jews.

Saul now decided to use his Roman name of Paul, and he has been known by that name ever since. He and Barnabas went first to Cyprus, where Barnabas had formerly lived, and they preached throughout the island.

The Roman Governor sent for them, because he was anxious to hear God's message. But a false prophet at his court opposed them.

Paul looked at the sorcerer. "You son of the devil and enemy of righteousness," he said. "When will you stop trying to distort the truth of God?"

The sorcerer was silenced, and the Governor became a believer.

Then Paul and Barnabas sailed away from Cyprus to the mainland, and preached to the Jews in the main cities.

Some believed, both Jews and non-Jews, but some violently opposed Paul and Barnabas, and plotted to kill them. But the two continued their journeys.

At one town, called Lystra, where they were preaching, a remarkable scene occurred. A man who had been lame from birth, and unable to walk, was listening to Paul's preaching. When Paul saw him he said loudly to him, "Stand up on your feet!" And the man stood up and walked!

Everyone was amazed, and began to think that their own gods had come down to earth. They even called Paul and Barnabas by the very names of their gods, and started to worship them. But the apostles cried out that they were men like everyone else.

"We are people, just like you are," they said. "Turn from these idols and serve the real God."

The crowd was quietened, but then some of the Jews from the other cities arrived. They worked up enemies against Paul, dragged him out of the city and began to stone him.

So Paul, who earlier had approved of the stoning of Stephen, was now himself stoned for the sake of the Gospel which he had once opposed. Paul's enemies struck him down so fiercely that when they left him they believed he was dead. But God was with him. He revived and was soon fit enough to go on to the next town.

Then he and Barnabas returned by the same route to the coast, visiting the towns where they had preached before, encouraging the Christians and appointing elders or leaders among them.

At last they returned to Antioch in Syria, after being away for two years on this first missionary journey.

For the next year Paul stayed at Antioch, except for a visit he made with Barnabas to the apostles at Jerusalem, where he described how greatly God had helped them both.

After a year, Paul and Barnabas decided that they must again visit the groups of believers throughout Asia Minor. Barnabas went with a young believer, named John Mark, to Cyprus, while Paul took another disciple, Silas, overland to the towns where they had previously preached.

This time there was no trouble, and they were able to encourage the Christians whom they met. Then God guided them across Asia to the sea-port of Troas.

At Troas, Paul dreamed that a man from Macedonia was speaking to him. "Come over to Macedonia and help us," the man said. So they sailed across to Macedonia in Northern Greece, and arrived at Philippi, the chief city.

At Philippi they found a group of believers who met for worship beside the river. The leader of this group was a lady called Lydia, who immediately invited Paul and Silas to stay at her house.

Paul and Silas began to preach in Philippi, but they found that a girl possessed of an evil spirit was following them. Wherever they went, she cried out after them.

This went on for some days, until Paul spoke to the spirit within her and said, "I command you in the name of Jesus Christ to come out of her." The spirit left her, and the girl was normal again.

But the girl's masters were angry, for the girl had brought them much money by foretelling the future. They seized Paul and Silas, dragged them into the market-place and charged them with causing a disturbance.

Paul and Silas were ordered to be flogged, and afterwards they were thrown into prison and their feet firmly fixed.

Paul and Silas knew that as faithful believers in Jesus Christ, they would have to endure hardship. So after praying to God, they began to sing hymns praising Him, while all the other prisoners listened in wonder. Suddenly about midnight there was a violent earthquake. The prison shook, the doors flew open and all the chains came away from the wall.

The jailer, thinking that all his prisoners had escaped, was about to kill himself. Then Paul shouted, "Do not kill yourself—we are all here!"

The jailer fell down at their feet and exclaimed, "Sirs, what must I do to be saved?"

"Believe in the Lord Jesus," they replied, "then you will be saved."

So the jailer was converted and baptised, together with his whole family. Although it was the middle of the night, he took them to his house, washed their wounds where they had been beaten, and gave them food.

The next morning Paul and Silas were released, and they received an apology from the magistrates. So they returned to the house of Lydia and gave thanks to God in prayer.

Then they moved on to the next town, Thessalonica. They preached that Jesus had risen from the dead and was indeed God's Messiah. A great many Greeks believed, but some of the Jews were angry, and exclaimed, "These men who have turned the world upside down have now come here too!"

Paul and Silas now had two companions: Timothy, who became Paul's chief assistant, and Luke, a Greek doctor, who wrote a Gospel and the Acts of the Apostles, which tells the life story of Paul.

While Silas and Timothy stayed with the Christians in Macedonia, Paul and Luke sailed to Athens, the capital of Greece and the centre of a great and ancient civilisation.

Athens was a famous centre of learning. Here wise men met and disputed and debated among the many magnificent buildings and temples.

Paul was worried by the fact that idols were openly worshipped. So he preached to the Jews in the synagogue and to the Gentiles in the market-place, stating that Jesus had risen from the dead. Some of the learned men at Athens heard about his preaching.

"What is this upstart saying?" they exclaimed, and they invited him to speak to their Council on Mars Hill.

Paul told them that he had seen an altar on which were written the words 'TO THE UNKNOWN GOD'. "This God," he said, "whom you worship without knowing, I shall tell you about." So he preached to them about Jesus and the Resurrection.

Some laughed at him, some were undecided, but a few became believers. Then Paul moved on to Corinth.

At Corinth, Paul took up again his old trade of tent-making, which he had learned as a young boy. He did this to earn some money for his food and lodging. He stayed with two Christian Jews who were also tent-makers, Aquila and his wife Priscilla. Paul preached every Sabbath, and a large number of people became Christians.

There was still opposition, but God encouraged Paul in a vision. "Have no fear," he was told. "Go on preaching and let no-one silence you. I am with you and no-one shall hurt you. There are many of My people in this city."

So Paul stayed for a year and a half, preaching and writing letters to groups of believers in the other cities he had visited.

Then he returned to Antioch, after taking Aquila and Priscilla as far as Ephesus to instruct the Christians there.

Paul was a very brave believer in Jesus Christ. He had been stoned, beaten, imprisoned and left for dead, yet he still went on with the task which he knew God had given him—spreading the good news about Jesus as far and wide as he could.

Soon he decided to set off on his third missionary journey. He started off the same way as before, overland to Lystra, Derbe, and the other towns of Asia Minor. He visited the groups of believers, encouraging them to stand firm in the faith.

Then he went on to Ephesus, where there was a large and growing number of Christians, although some of them knew only very little about Jesus—for there were no church buildings, no clergymen and, as yet, no New Testament.

Paul stayed in Ephesus for two years, teaching, preaching and healing the sick. Then came trouble.

The people of Ephesus used to worship a statue called Diana. Some silversmiths earned their living by making images of Diana in silver and selling them.

So many people were turning to Christianity that this trade grew less. The silversmiths gathered a crowd together, and claimed that their goddess was greater than Paul's God.

The excited crowd became worked up against the Christians. They found some believers and dragged them into the arena. Paul wanted to help the Christians, but the disciples would not let him in case he was injured.

The crowd kept up an endless shout for two whole hours: "Great is Diana of the Ephesians! Great is Diana of the Ephesians!" Finally the Town Clerk came, spoke to them, and calmed them down.

So order was restored and a serious riot avoided. Despite this violence, the number of Christians continued to grow.

Paul then travelled back through Macedonia and Greece, helping Christians wherever he went. On the way home with Luke and his companions, he spent a week at Troas. On the evening before they sailed, Paul spoke to the Christians in an upper room for a long time.

The room was crowded and hot, and a young man named Eutychus, who was sitting on the window-sill, fell fast asleep. Gradually he slipped and fell right out of the window, from the third storey to the ground.

Everyone thought he must have been killed, including Luke the doctor. But Paul bent over him and said, "Don't worry, he is alive!" He helped the young man to his feet and, greatly relieved, they took him home alive.

Paul talked with the Christians right through the night. Then in the morning he set off by sea for Palestine.

Back in Palestine, Paul heard that there was another plot to kill him. Some Jews believed that he was preaching against their religion and saying that there was no longer any need to obey the Law of Moses.

The Christians begged him not to go up to Jerusalem, as his life was in danger. However, Paul would not be persuaded, saying, "I am quite prepared to die for the sake of Jesus Christ."

So off to Jerusalem he went. Here the disciples advised him to show himself in the temple for a week, as a sign that he still observed the Law of Moses.

This he did, but on the sixth day, some of the Jews from Asia saw him, seized him, and stirred up the crowd against him.

They dragged him outside the temple, and tried to kill him.

Paul would certainly have been killed if the Roman soldiers, hearing the uproar, had not come and protected him. Paul persuaded them to let him speak to the crowd.

He told the crowd how Jesus Christ had appeared to him on the road to Damascus, but the crowd did not believe him, and many cried out, "Kill him! Kill him! He must not live!" So the Romans arrested Paul and took him into their barracks to keep him out of danger.

Forty Jews then made a vow that they would neither eat nor drink until Paul had been killed. They plotted to hide beside a path along which they knew he would pass.

But Paul's nephew heard of the plot and ran to tell Paul, who sent him to the Captain. The young lad told the Captain about the plot to kill Paul. The Captain thanked him and warned him not to tell anyone else.

Paul was an important person, and a Roman citizen, so he could not be kept under arrest without a proper trial. It was important that he should be taken safely out of Jerusalem. The Captain decided to send him, under escort, to the Roman Governor at Caesarea. He ordered 400 soldiers and 70 horsemen to take Paul to Felix, the Governor, by night.

Felix heard his case, but delayed making any decision. He did not believe that Paul had done wrong, but to please the Jews he kept him a prisoner for two whole years.

Then a new Governor, Festus, arrived. He heard Paul's case, and the case against him. But Paul soon realised that the new Governor also wanted to please the Jews, and might have him executed, so he decided to appeal to Caesar, in Rome.

"Very well," said Festus. "You have appealed to Caesar. Then to Caesar you shall go!"

Then Paul, with Luke and other companions, was taken under escort to a ship which was sailing to Asia. On arrival they changed to a large sailing vessel going to Italy.

But the wind was boisterous and against them, and progress was slow. They put into a harbour at Crete, and Paul warned that further sailing would be dangerous.

However, the captain decided to sail out to a better port at the far end of Crete. Soon after they had set sail a tremendous gale blew up. The ship was driven out to sea, and buffeted violently by wind and waves.

The storm drove them on for several days. No-one ate anything, and all the others gave up hope of being saved.

But Paul was encouraged by God, and helped everyone. "Keep your spirits up!" he said. "No life will be lost, even if we lose the ship."

The storm blew for fourteen days and nights. Then, at last, they realised one night that land was near. While they waited for day to break, Paul spoke to them again.

"Take some food, I beg you. No-one will be lost." He himself took some bread, gave thanks, and ate it. Then everyone began to eat again.

At daybreak they found themselves in a bay. The ship was blown against a reef and began to break up. Everyone jumped into the sea, and swam or floated on wood to the shore. No-one was lost, as God had promised Paul.

The land they reached was Malta, and here the whole party of sailors, soldiers and prisoners stayed for some time. Paul was able to heal the father of the Roman Governor and many other people also. After three months they boarded another ship sailing for Italy.

And so they came to Rome—capital city and centre of the great Roman Empire. The Christians there met Paul and Luke and warmly welcomed them. Paul was allowed to live in a house, with a Roman soldier to guard him.

Paul was not idle—he could never be that! He received many visitors and preached to them, explaining all about Jesus and His Kingdom. He wrote letters, especially to the Christians in the churches he had started, including those at Philippi and Ephesus.

Paul remained in Rome for two years. Luke, in his writings, says—"He received every one that went in unto him, preaching the Kingdom of God and teaching the things concerning the Lord Jesus Christ with all boldness."

Eventually he was brought before the Emperor, who ordered him to be executed. So he died, as he had lived, in the service of Jesus Christ.

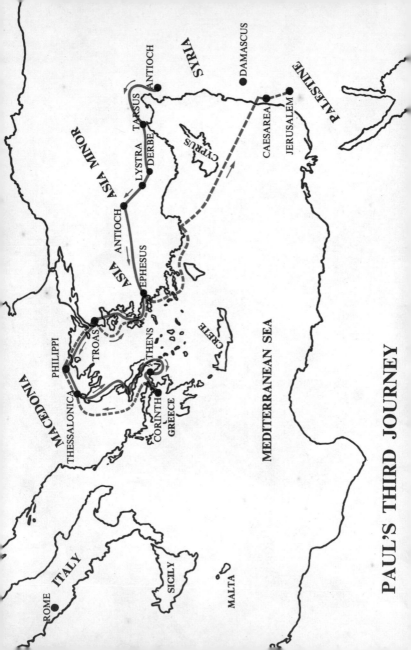

PAUL'S THIRD JOURNEY